Dear Parent:
Your child's love of reading starts here!

Every child learns to read in a different way and at his or her own speed. Some go back and forth between reading levels and read favorite books again and again. Others read through each level in order. You can help your young reader improve and become more confident by encouraging his or her own interests and abilities. From books your child reads with you to the first books he or she reads alone, there are I Can Read Books for every stage of reading:

SHARED READING
Basic language, word repetition, and whimsical illustrations, ideal for sharing with your emergent reader

BEGINNING READING
Short sentences, familiar words, and simple concepts for children eager to read on their own

READING WITH HELP
Engaging stories, longer sentences, and language play for developing readers

READING ALONE
Complex plots, challenging vocabulary, and high-interest topics for the independent reader

ADVANCED READING
Short paragraphs, chapters, and exciting themes for the perfect bridge to chapter books

I Can Read Books have introduced children to the joy of reading since 1957. Featuring award-winning authors and illustrators and a fabulous cast of beloved characters, I Can Read Books set the standard for beginning readers.

A lifetime of discovery begins with the magical words "I Can Read!"

Visit www.icanread.com for information
on enriching your child's reading experience.

At Home

I Can Read!™

READING
3
ALONE

in a New Land

Joan Sandin

HarperCollins*Publishers*

For all immigrants
past and present.
May they feel at home
in their new land.
—J.S.

HarperCollins®, ☎®, and I Can Read Book® are trademarks of HarperCollins Publishers Inc.

At Home in a New Land Copyright © 2007 by Joan Sandin All rights reserved. No part of this book may be used or reproduced in any manner whatsoever without written permission except in the case of brief quotations embodied in critical articles and reviews. Printed in the United States of America. For information address HarperCollins Children's Books, a division of HarperCollins Publishers, 1350 Avenue of the Americas, New York, NY 10019. www.harpercollinschildrens.com

Library of Congress Cataloging-in-Publication Data is available.
ISBN-10: 0-06-058077-1 (trade bdg.) — ISBN-13: 978-0-06-058077-3 (trade bdg.)
ISBN-10: 0-06-058078-X (lib. bdg.) — ISBN-13: 978-0-06-058078-0 (lib. bdg.)

1 2 3 4 5 6 7 8 9 10 ❖ First Edition

CONTENTS

Swedish words in the story

gode   (goo-deh) good

Gud   (Giood) God

nog   (noog)   enough

tack   (tahk)   thank you

I. Minnesota

Carl Erik opened his eyes

and looked around the strange room.

It was not a dream.

The long, hard journey from Sweden

was really over.

He was in Minnesota!

His aunt Sara was smiling at him.

"You must be very hungry," she said.

She buttered a thick slab

of hot cornbread for him.

She poured him a cup of milk.

Carl Erik ate and drank eagerly.

It was so long since he had tasted
anything so good.

Anna Stina moved closer to her cousin.

She had not seen him for two years,

since the day she left for America.

"Is it true you ate bread
made from tree bark?" she asked.
"Yes," said Carl Erik.
"We were starving in Sweden.
It was all we had."

"Well, now you will eat wheat bread, and cornbread, and maple syrup," said Anna Stina happily.

"And you will live here with us until you build your own cabin. Come, I will show you around."

Carl Erik followed his cousin outside.

"Will we be neighbors?" he asked her.

"I think we will," she said, smiling.

"Pappa knows about some good land

just across the lake.

He is taking your father there now!"

II. Free Homestead Land

Carl Erik's father jumped down

from the wagon.

He waved a paper in the air.

"I have filed a claim," he shouted.

"On 160 acres of free Minnesota land!
All we have to do is build a cabin
and clear some of the land," he said.
"In five years it will be ours!"

13

"There is work at the logging camp,"
Uncle Axel told his wife.
"They are paying a dollar a day!
I could buy the horses we need,
and Anders could earn enough to buy
nails and windows to build his cabin.
But we would be gone a long time."
"We will manage," said Aunt Sara.

The day the men left for the camp,
Carl Erik's father took him aside.
"While we are away," he said,
"you will be the man of the house.
You must help the women
and take care of the traps
so there will be meat for the table."

Carl Erik was proud

to be the man of the house,

but with his father and uncle gone,

there was so much work to do.

Every day he had to milk the cow,

feed the animals,

and carry in wood and water.

Sometimes Jonas went with him.

Every night Carl Erik set the traps.

Every morning he found them empty.

"Don't worry," Aunt Sara told him.

"We have plenty of potatoes."

III. School

The children worked fast
digging up all the potatoes.
School would start in a few days.

"We have no schoolhouse here,"
Aunt Sara told Carl Erik's mother.
"School moves from farm to farm.
It will be at the Olssons' this term."

It was a long walk to the Olsson farm,
around the lake and through the woods.
"Look," Anna Stina said one morning.
She pointed at a tepee by the lake.
"Our nearest neighbors live there."
Carl Erik gasped.

Miss Lind was waiting at the door.

Carl Erik pulled off his cap.

He bowed to his new teacher

and greeted her politely in Swedish.

"But Indians live in tepees!" he said.

"And Indians scalp people!"

"Where did you hear that?" she asked.

"That is what people in Sweden say,"
Carl Erik said.

"Well, people around here say
the Ojibway are good neighbors,"
said his cousin.

He heard someone laugh inside.

"This is an American school,"

said Miss Lind.

"Here we speak only English."

"Sit here," said Miss Lind.

"You will share a book with Ralph."

Carl Erik had learned to read in Sweden,

but the letters in Ralph's book

did not make any words he knew.

He stared at the strange words.

"Dumb Swede," whispered Ralph.

When Miss Lind turned her back,

he grabbed one of Carl Erik's shoes.

He tossed it out the open window.

Carl Erik felt his face grow hot.

He swung at Ralph.

Miss Lind spun around.

"NOG!" she shouted.

"ENOUGH!"

Carl Erik had to stay in at recess.

Miss Lind is not fair, he thought.

But then he noticed something.

Ralph was not playing with the others.

He was chopping wood.

Miss Lind was punishing him, too.

A boy came over to the window.

"Ralph's real name is Rolf," he said.

"He is from Sweden, just like all of us.

He has forgotten how it feels

to be new in America, but I have not.

My name is Henrik Olsson—Henry.

Here, have some of my maple sugar."

"Tack!" said Carl Erik. "Thank you!"

Carl Erik knew he was not dumb.

He would show that bully Rolf!

He was already good with numbers,

and he would work hard on his English.

Miss Lind let him borrow a book.

He read for Anna Stina

on the long walks home.

He even read when he did his chores.

One day he read for his mother.

She understood only a few words,

but she smiled and told him

he was as clever as Anna Stina.

"Too bad you are not so clever
with your traps," said Jonas.
"Never you mind," said Carl Erik.
But Jonas was right about the traps.
Even when Carl Erik moved them
or tried different bait,
he never caught anything.

Some man of the house he was!
What would his father and uncle say?

IV. The Visitor

The ten-week term was almost over.

Carl Erik was now reading English

as well as Ralph was.

Miss Lind was so pleased,

she let him sit next to Henrik.

The days grew colder and darker.

Snow lay thick on the ground.

The men had been gone

for more than three months.

One morning everyone went to town

except Carl Erik.

He stayed home to tend the fire

and take care of the animals.

He was putting a log on the fire
when suddenly the room grew dark.
Something was covering the window.
Carl Erik looked closer and gasped.
He saw a face looking in at him!
Carl Erik froze with fear.
An Indian!

The door opened slowly.

The Indian strode across the room,

over to the fire to warm himself.

Then the man moved toward the door.

He signaled to Carl Erik to follow.

Was the Indian going to scalp him?

Carl Erik could hardly breathe,

but he tried not to show his fear.

He followed the Indian outside.

The man picked up some stones
and buried them in the ground.
What is he doing? thought Carl Erik.
Then the man dug up the stones
and pretended to eat them.
Suddenly Carl Erik understood!
The Indian wanted their potatoes!
What should he do?

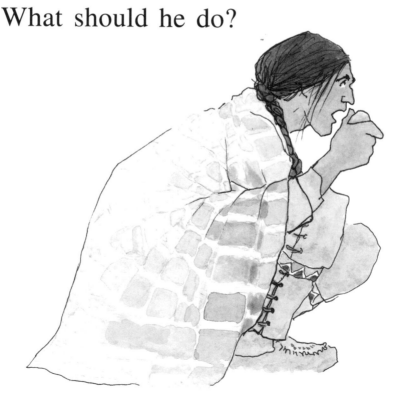

Carl Erik knew that in Sweden
good neighbors helped each other,
and Anna Stina had told him
the Ojibway were good neighbors.

He led the way to the potato cellar.

The Indian filled his blanket.

He said something to Carl Erik,

patted his blond hair, and laughed.

Then he slipped back into the forest.

That night Carl Erik told Aunt Sara
what he had done.

"You did the right thing," she said.

"You shared with our neighbors."

V. The Gift

The school term was finally over.

Christmas was coming!

The women were getting ready
just the way they did in Sweden—
making candles, scouring the pots,
scrubbing the floor, and baking.

Carl Erik and Anna Stina had found
a perfect little tree in the woods.
Jonas went with them to chop it down.
The cousins heard shouts and looked up.

A tall Indian on a toboggan
was weaving down Big Hill.
Two boys were holding on behind him,
laughing and shouting.

"It is Deer Hunter and his sons,"
Anna Stina told her cousins.
"Oh! That is the Indian who came
for the potatoes!" said Carl Erik.
"Why was I ever afraid of him?"

That night Carl Erik's mother
opened the big "America trunk,"
filled with treasures from home.
She took out some paper hearts.
"Do you remember these?" she asked.
"Oh yes!" cried Jonas. "I made them!
May I hang them on our tree?"
"Of course you may," said Aunt Sara.
"And then Anna Stina can show you
how to pop corn and string it,
the way the Americans do."

Carl Erik heard a noise outside.

Could it be his father and Uncle Axel?

Carl Erik's heart beat faster

as he opened the door and looked out.

Moonlight sparkled on the snow.

He saw someone in the distance,

disappearing into the dark woods.

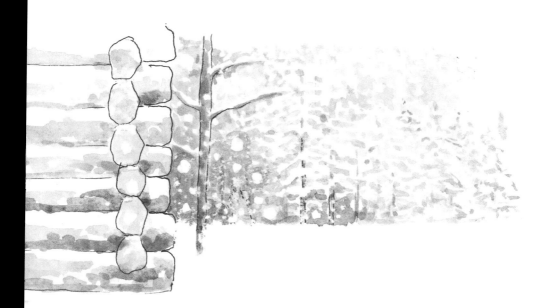

His foot bumped against something.

It was a big slab of meat!

"Where did this come from?" he said.

Aunt Sara laughed and hugged him.

"Oh, Carl Erik, can't you guess?

You shared with our good neighbors,

and now they have shared with us.

What a Christmas feast we will have!"

VI. Christmas

The cabin smelled of pine branches,

freshly baked wheat bread,

rice pudding, and cinnamon.

"It smells like Swedish Christmas."

Mamma sighed.

"What a pity Anders and Axel

cannot share this feast with us."

She put the platter of roast meat

in the center of the table.

Aunt Sara led the family in prayer.

"*Tack, gode Gud*, for keeping us safe.

Please bring us all together soon . . ."

Suddenly the cabin door flew open.

In blew a gust of cold wind

and two men covered with ice and snow.

"Look!" cried one of the men.

"We have died and come to Heaven!"

"Anders! Axel!" cried Aunt Sara.

The men shook snow from their coats.

The children helped them

pull off their wet boots.

Everybody was hugging

and laughing

and talking

at the same time.

Then Axel saw the big platter of meat.

"What is this?" he asked, surprised.

"Roast venison!" said his wife.

"You may thank Carl Erik

for that."

"What?" said Uncle Axel, laughing.

"Did the boy get a deer

in one of his squirrel traps?"

Carl Erik blushed and looked down.

He thought of his empty traps

and the potatoes he had given away.

What if his father and Uncle Axel

were angry with him?

While they ate, Aunt Sara told the men
all that had happened.

"Carl Erik," said his uncle,
"look at me."

Carl Erik slowly raised his head.

Uncle Axel was smiling!

"Well, man of the house," he said,

"you have made us very proud."

"Off to bed now," said Aunt Sara.

"But Mamma," said Anna Stina,

"we have to hang up our stockings!"

"But mine are not wet," said Jonas.

"You will see!" laughed Anna Stina.

In the morning, Jonas woke Carl Erik.
"Look! There are apples and sweets
in our stockings!" cried Jonas.

It was still dark outside.

The men were hitching up the oxen.

They had filled the sleigh with hay.

"Climb in!" shouted Uncle Axel,

tucking them in under a bearskin robe.

Off they went through the deep snow,

the jingle of their sleigh bells

the only sound in the dark woods.

As they came near the town,

Carl Erik saw the flickering light

from the torches

stuck in the snow outside the church.

He heard the voices inside singing

the old Swedish Christmas hymns.

He saw his new friend Henrik.

With his family tucked in around him,

Carl Erik felt warm and happy.

He felt at home in his new land.

Author Note

During the "hunger years" of 1868 and '69, more than 50,000 Swedes came to America. Most went westward to find jobs in the cities or to farm the free land created by the new Homestead Act. Many settled in Minnesota, which reminded them of Sweden with its woods and lakes. Often they had friends or family there who helped them. By 1870 some 20,000 Swedish-speaking immigrants had built their own communities and churches in Minnesota. However, in the American schools, the immigrant children were required to speak English, both in the classroom and on the playground. In time, the Swedes, like other immigrant groups, adopted the language and customs of their new land, but they never entirely forgot those of their mother country.